THE DINOSAUR THAT POOPED A PIRATE!

Check out Danny and Dinosaur in more adventures:

PICTURE BOOKS:

The Dinosaur that Pooped Christmas!
The Dinosaur that Pooped a Planet!
The Dinosaur that Pooped the Past!
The Dinosaur that Pooped the Bed!
The Dinosaur that Pooped a Princess!

AND FOR YOUNGER READERS:

The Dinosaur that Pooped Daddy!
The Dinosaur that Pooped a Rainbow!

For Buzz, Buddy and Max – T.F.
I would like to thank RhymeZone – D.P.
For young pirate Beau – G.P.

RED FOX

UK | USA | Canada | Ireland | Australia
India | New Zealand | South Africa

Red Fox is part of the Penguin Random House group of companies
whose addresses can be found at global.penguinrandomhouse.com.

www.penguin.co.uk   www.puffin.co.uk   www.ladybird.co.uk

Penguin
Random House
UK

First published 2020
001

Copyright © Tom Fletcher and Dougie Poynter, 2020
Illustrated by Garry Parsons
The moral right of the authors has been asserted

Printed in China

A CIP catalogue record for this book is available from the British Library

ISBN: 978–1–782–95544–3

All correspondence to:
Red Fox, Penguin Random House Children's
One Embassy Gardens, 8 Viaduct Gardens, London SW11 7BW

THE DINOSAUR THAT POOPED A PIRATE!

Tom Fletcher and Dougie Poynter

Illustrated by Garry Parsons

RED FOX

Danny and Dinosaur sailed out to sea
On a ship that was crooked and old.
With a map in Dan's hand of a faraway land
Where a pirate had hidden his gold!

They sailed all day with nothing for lunch –
Not even a sniff of a snack.
They searched high and low, but found nothing and so
They were going to have to turn back!

But just when it looked like they'd have to go home
Danny held up a scope to his eye . . .
And on the horizon he spotted Skull Island
And so, "Land ahoy!" Danny cried.

"Yo-ho!
Land ahoy,
land ahoy!"
Danny cried.

Danny hoisted the sail, Dino steered with his tail
And they anchored their ship by the shore.

"This is it!" Danny cheered. "The treasure is near!"
And they jumped off the ship to explore.

But while Danny studied the map to the gold
Dinosaur's tummy was rumbling.
"There's no time for that - we must follow the map!
Tell that belly of yours to stop grumbling!"

They followed the map
   through the wet sloppy mud
To a place known as Crocodile Cave.
   "Let's go in!" Danny cried. "There's treasure to find.
   We're going to have to be brave!

Yo-ho!
We're going to
have to be brave!"

Danny crept past the crocs, with their razor-sharp teeth
That were open and ready to crunch.

His nose in the map, Danny didn't look back
To see Dinosaur eat them for lunch!

Next on the map was a mermaid lagoon -
Mermaids magically tempted them in.
Danny put on his trunks, and he felt like a hunk,
Saying, "Dinosaur, come for a swim!

Yo-ho!
You have to come
in for a swim!"

But Dinosaur knew Dan was under a spell,
  For this place was too good to be true.
So, before Dan could say that he wanted to stay,
            Dinosaur drank the lagoon!

Next on the map was a grand pirate ship
That was stranded in Barnacle Bay.
And the pirates on board were incredibly bored
Until Danny heard one of them say,

"Yo-ho!
There are trespassers
coming this way!"

They loaded their cannons and readied the plank –
These swashbuckling pirates were angry.
But hornswoggling crooks with no teeth and sharp hooks
Are no match for a Dino that's HANGRY!

Danny studied the map and
they followed the trail,
Crossed the bridge made
of skeleton bones,

Charmed the
venomous snake,

Swam with sharks in the lake,
Took a selfie with
Old Davy Jones,

Leapt a pit full of spikes,
    cartwheeled over some crabs,

Flew with parrots down Buccaneer Falls.
    But with eyes on the prize
Dan did not realize
    That his Dino first-mate ate them all!

Yo-ho!
    His Dino first-mate
    ate them all!

Now, reader, beware - our sailors have reached
The most treacherous part of this tale.
For the X on the map, where the treasure was at,
Was inside the mouth of a WHALE!

"I'm not scared!' Dan declared as he ventured inside.
And where Danny went, Dinosaur followed . . .

But the map was a trap and the whale went SNAP
And both Danny and Dino were swallowed!

Oh no!
Both Danny and Dino
were swallowed!

There was treasure all right, jewels and diamonds galore –
They were sparkling as bright as can be.
But there's no use in gold if you're stuck growing old
In a whale on the bed of the sea.

Yo-ho!
So Dino had
treasure for tea!

It was sticky and icky
and smelled very fishy

And so Danny
started to cry.

Their only way out was
through the whale's spout,
And they couldn't reach –
it was too high!

But with pirates and mermaids inside of its gut
The dinosaur knew what to do.

After such a big feast,
To escape from the beast
The dinosaur needed to . . .

They blew out of the spout twenty leagues in the sky
And escaped from the whale in a flash.
The poo-powered pair plastered poop everywhere
As the dinosaur's bum made a splash!

He dropped off the parrots at Buccaneer Falls
And plopped the crocs back in their cave.
The mermaids were pooed into Mermaid Lagoon -
Danny blew them a kiss and they waved.

Yo-ho!
He blew them a kiss
and they waved!

Skeleton bones and Old Davy Jones
came tumbling out of his bottom.
The lake that he drank
was now brown and it stank
Like a nappy that had been forgotten.

He pooed piles of pirates in Barnacle Bay
Then squeezed out their ship for good measure.
They were brown head to toe and a little cross, so . . .
The dinosaur pooped out the treasure!

Hooray! The dinosaur pooped out the treasure!

They crashed on the beach where this journey began,
The hunt for the treasure had beat them.
"Let's go home!" Danny cried, just relieved they'd survived
And the two of them hadn't been eaten!

Dino hoisted his tail and his wind filled the sails
And they headed towards the horizon.
They stood on the deck and would never forget
The adventure they had on Skull Island . . .

Yo-ho! Then Dinosaur pooped out a diamond!